Butterflies Below Zero

Written by Stella Santa Cruz
Illustrated by Paula Hatton

Contents

For learning solutions, visit cengage.com.au

Meet the Characters

Lucas Morpho

A butterfly expert.

Lucia Morpho

A butterfly expert's wife.

Dr Stinson

A butterfly expert's boss.

Kelly Morpho

A butterfly expert's twin daughter.

Fifi Morpho

A butterfly expert's other twin daughter.

Dear Reader

Here's a great idea for a tropical holiday without even going to the airport! I got the idea when I visited a butterfly sanctuary in a very cold part of the country. It was freezing outside – but in the sanctuary, hundreds of brightly coloured butterflies were enjoying beautiful hot weather. Lucky them!

Stella Santa Cruz

Author

The Morpho House

1. Hallway
2. Lounge
3. Kitchen
4. Lucas and Lucia's room
5. Kelly's room
6. Fifi's room

A Butterfly Expert

Lucas Morpho loved butterflies. He studied them carefully. He collected them eagerly. He taught about them enthusiastically. Like a proud parent, he watched over the eggs, caterpillars and cocoons in his lab until they turned into butterflies.

On a trip to South America, Lucas Morpho had even found a new kind of butterfly. He named it after his wife and twin girls.

"It's called *Papilio luciakellyfifius*," he said, showing them a photo.

His wife, Lucia, who had been hoping Lucas would bring her some pretty jewellery when he returned, smiled. Kelly and Fifi, who had hoped their dad would bring back some ponchos for them, rolled their eyes.

"Thanks Dad," they said.

Winter arrived early, with grey clouds and icy winds. Lucas Morpho didn't like winter. With snow on the ground, there were no butterflies to be found. Kelly and Fifi didn't like it either. It was no fun going to school on frosty, below-zero mornings.

"We need a holiday," Lucia said one morning, as she packed the girls' lunches.

"What a good idea," said Lucas, who was doing the dishes.

The twins couldn't believe their luck.

"A holiday?" squeaked Kelly.

"Where shall we go?" asked Fifi.

"They have some great butterflies in Tierra del Fuego," said Lucas. "We could have a great holiday studying …"

"No, no, no," said Lucia. "I mean a *proper* holiday. Somewhere hot, where we can drink juice, and lie on deckchairs in our bathers reading books."

"But Tierra del Fuego is not so bad over summer," said Lucas. "And …"

"No," said Lucia firmly. Lucas looked at the twins, who were also shaking their heads. He knew he was beaten.

"OK," he said. "A tropical holiday, with juice, deckchairs, bathers and books."

His family beamed.

"Can they be butterfly books?" he chuckled, ducking a hail of teatowels, toast crusts and slippers.

2 Some Bad News

Within a week, the Morpho family holiday was all planned. Brochures were read and a warm island resort was chosen. Flights were booked. Dusty passports were found. Long-lost bathers came out of drawers. Lucia, Kelly and Fifi even learned some words and phrases.

"*Sha-buli!*" said Fifi, which was the word for "welcome".

"*Canda shiba harimas?*" said Kelly, which meant "How are you?"

Then, the week before the holiday, Lucas came home with some bad news.

"We can't go," he said glumly. "The university is closing my lab."

"What?" gasped Lucia, Kelly and Fifi. "Why?"

"They decided that they need more lawyers, doctors and accountants," sighed Lucas. "Butterflies just aren't important enough."

"But that's awful," said Lucia. "You're a famous butterfly expert. They can't just close you down."

"They can and they have," said Lucas, looking very sad.

The family sat at the table, wondering what to do. Then Lucia stood up.

"I don't know what will happen to us," she said, "but I do know we'll get through this. And I do know what we're going to do now."

Lucas, Kelly and Fifi looked at her with wide eyes.

"We're going to have a big family hug, and then we'll sleep on it. In the morning, we'll have some new ideas. Then we'll know what to do."

It was the best idea. And she was right.

When Lucas leapt out of bed the next morning, he was so excited he almost took the blankets and Lucia out with him.

"I've got it!" he said.

"Got what?" yawned Lucia. She looked at the alarm clock and then remembered what had happened last night.

"A plan!" Lucas called from the bathroom.

Lucia went to wake Kelly and Fifi. When everyone was ready for breakfast, they sat at the table. Lucas was already there.

"OK, Dad, what's the plan?" said Kelly sleepily.

"You said you wanted a proper holiday; somewhere tropical, where we could drink juice and lie on deckchairs in our bathers reading books. And that's exactly what we're going to do."

The twins and their mother looked at each other.

"But, Dad," said Fifi. "What about the lab?"

"Never mind that," said Lucas with a wave of his hand. "We are more important. I promised you a holiday and a holiday is what we shall have." Then Lucas told them his plan.

At first they were ASTONISHED. Then they were AGHAST. Then they were AMAZED. And finally, they started to smile. It was a crazy plan, but it might just be the best tropical holiday ever!

3 A Crazy Plan

A large van with the lab logo on it backed up the driveway, until Lucas yelled "Stop!" Grinning, he helped the van driver unload the crates and boxes and large items marked "Fragile". Slowly, the lounge and the dining room and the hallway and the bedrooms and the bathroom started to fill up.

Meanwhile, Lucia was on the phone to a plant shop.

Slowly, the lounge and the DINING ROOM AND THE hallway

"Are you sure?" asked the manager. "It is winter, you know."

But Lucia was insistent, and the manager agreed to make a special delivery.

After school, Kelly and Fifi went to get some books. They even got a copy of *Butterfly Monthly* for their dad.

That night, when everyone was together, Lucas rubbed his hands together and said, "OK, team, let's put this plan into action."

and the *bedrooms* and **the** bathroom started to fill up.

Kelly and Fifi raced around the house collecting heaters and making sure all the windows and doors were tightly closed. Lucia turned the outside light on. Outside were all the plant shop's palms and ferns and bromeliads and tropical hanging baskets. And Lucas started unwrapping all the items from the butterfly lab that the university said they no longer wanted.

"Just over there," he said, as Lucia carried in a beautiful, lush palm tree.

"A little warmer, please," he instructed, as the twins set up the heaters.

"Ah, just like the tropics," he murmured, as the house grew warmer and warmer.

"Don't forget the water, darling," he said.

Fifi filled up saucers of water and placed them in front of the heaters. The windows steamed up. Lucas smiled.

The living room was filled with ferns, palms and bromeliads. Lucas set up some deckchairs, checked the refrigerator, and winked at his daughters. This was going to be the best holiday ever – and they wouldn't even have to leave home!

Lucas set up the incubators, and carefully checked that all the cocoons and pupae were warm and safe.

The living room was looking and feeling like a tropical paradise.

"Now what?" asked Fifi.

"Now," said Lucas, "it's bedtime."

The next morning, everyone was tired. It had been hard to get to sleep.

"It's just as if we've all been on a plane overnight," said Lucas with a wink. The family stood outside the lounge. "Are we ready?"

The twins nodded, and Lucia smiled. "We're ready," she said.

"Welcome to our tropical holiday!" beamed Lucas, as he swung open the door.

An incredible sight met their eyes. They were speechless.

A burst of humid, warm air swept out from the living room. Palm trees and ferns filled every corner and the smell of tropical flowers filled the air. In the centre of the room, four bright deckchairs awaited the holidaymakers.

But that was not the most amazing thing. Hundreds of newly hatched tropical butterflies fluttered and drifted around the room. Bright blues and greens, deep reds and golds, blacks and purples filled the air like confetti. Butterflies brushed past the twins' ears and shoulders, and landed on their heads.

Lucia looked at the tropical scene in total wonder. It was beautiful. She gave her husband a huge hug.

"Careful, darling," he said. He gently waved a black and red butterfly away. "You almost squashed a *Papilio eurymedon*, you know."

Lucia nudged Lucas in the ribs. "You know, Lucas, this is far prettier than any jewellery you could ever have bought me," she said. "Thank you."

“And these colours are so much better than any ponchos we’ve ever seen,” said the twins. “Thanks, Dad. This is cool.”

While Lucas went to get the fresh juice out of the refrigerator, Lucia, Kelly and Fifi flopped into their deckchairs. It was so warm in the living room that, if they closed their eyes, they could imagine they were in the tropics somewhere. Better still, when they opened their eyes, they could still imagine it!

“This is the best holiday,” said Kelly.

4 A Visitor

Later that day, as the family sipped their juices, read their books and watched the butterflies swooping and fluttering, there was a knock at the door.

"That must be room service," Lucas joked, pulling himself out of his deckchair. He had been reading his copy of *Butterfly Monthly*.

Checking for stray butterflies, he carefully opened the door, and got a huge surprise – but not as big as the surprise his visitor got.

"Mr Morpho?" exclaimed Dr Stinson, who was in charge of the university. He looked at Lucas's shorts, and wondered if losing his job had sent him mad. "Err, it is winter, you know."

"Oh, this?" chuckled Lucas. "No, no, no, it's just …"

But Dr Stinson was ignoring him. He watched incredulously as tropical butterflies wafted through the living room door and into the kitchen.

He pointed. His mouth opened. And then he saw the rest of the family lounging on deckchairs reading books. He was speechless.

"Would you like to come in?" said Lucas.

"I … I …" said Dr Stinson.

"*Sha-buli*!" said Fifi, which was the word for "welcome".

"*Canda shiba harimas*?" said Kelly, which meant "How are you?"

"I did check that it was OK to borrow the lab equipment," explained Lucas. "I'll bring it back next week. When we close down."

But Dr Stinson was busy looking at a beautiful steely blue butterfly that was about to land on his nose. He loosened his tie, and turned to Lucas.

"This is amazing. Did you do all of this?"

"Well ..." Lucas began.

"We all helped," said the twins. "Would you like a juice?"

Dr Stinson held out his hand, and a red and gold butterfly sat on his palm.

"I wanted to talk to you about the lab." Dr Stinson turned to Lucas. "But now I'm having second thoughts. I think we could do something amazing with your idea."

"Really?" said Lucas. "What idea?"

"This idea," said Dr Stinson, looking around. "Imagine if we turned the lab into a tourist attraction," he went on. "It's below zero outside – but inside we could have a tropical butterfly house. That would be a great way for people to learn about butterflies – and it would keep the accountants happy!"

"You mean … you might consider butterflies?" asked Lucas. Lucia and the twins looked at Dr Stinson.

A *Papilio luciakellyfifius* flew up to Dr Stinson and landed on his shoulder.

Dr Stinson, who already knew that everyone in the cold, frosty city would just love to see these butterflies in a warm, tropical environment, nodded. "I don't see why not," he said. "Come to my office. We can talk about it tomorrow."

“I’m sorry,” said Lucas, “but as you see, I’m on holiday.”

“Well, come as soon as you get back,” said Dr Stinson with a smile.

After he left, Lucia suggested another big family hug, which was just the right thing to do – although they had to be very careful about the butterflies.

Lucas grinned and scratched his head.

“This has been the best holiday,” he said, and everyone nodded. “But do you think I should have suggested a cold-climate butterfly house? Like Tierra del Fuego?”

Lucas raised his eyebrows. "We could just leave the windows open and turn the fans on …"

"Dad!"

He ducked a hail of books, tea towels and fruit peel.

Life was back to normal – apart from the tropical paradise in the lounge.

THE END